Winnie AND Wilbur

BROOMSTICK ALERT

and other stories

Wilbur

Winnie the Witch

Wanda

The Head Teacher

The Little Ordinaries

Wayne

Mrs Parmar

Jerry the Giant

The Toof Fairy

The Shopkeeper

The Conductor

Wendy

Auntie Aggie

OXFORD
UNIVERSITY PRESS

Great Clarendon Street, Oxford OX2 6DP

Oxford University Press is a department of the University of Oxford.
It furthers the University's objective of excellence in research, scholarship,
and education by publishing worldwide. Oxford is a registered trade mark of
Oxford University Press in the UK and in certain other countries

Database right Oxford University Press (maker)

Winnie and Wilbur: Whizz-Bang Winnie first published as *Whizz-Bang Winnie* in 2008
Winnie and Wilbur: Mini Winnie first published as *Mini Winnie* in 2008
Winnie and Wilbur: Winnie Says Cheese first published as *Winnie Says Cheese* in 2009
Winnie and Wilbur: Broomstick Alert and Other Stories first published as
Absolutely Winnie! in 2013
This edition first published in 2017

British Library Cataloguing in Publication Data: data available

ISBN: 978-0-19-275847-7

1 3 5 7 9 10 8 6 4 2

Printed in Great Britain

Paper used in the production of this book is a natural,
recyclable product made from wood grown in sustainable forests.
The manufacturing process conforms to the environmental
regulations of the country of origin.

LAURA OWEN & KORKY PAUL

Winnie AND Wilbur

BROOMSTICK ALERT

and other stories

OXFORD
UNIVERSITY PRESS

CONTENTS

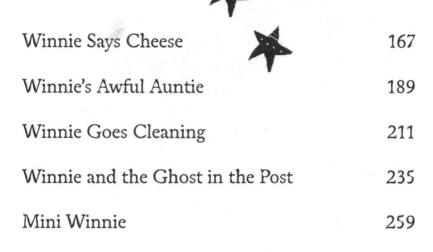

Hot Cross
WINNIE

Winnie's garden was as hot as a cauldron.
Wilbur lay under a rhubarb leaf with his
legs stretched and his tongue hanging out.
Along came Winnie wearing such dark
sunglasses that, **TRIP!**—

'Mrrrow!'

'Whoops! Blooming cat!' said Winnie,
rubbing her nose.

'Mrrow-ow-ow!' said Wilbur.

'Well, I'm hot too, you know!' said Winnie.

'I'm a hot cross witch and you're a hot cross cat. We need to cool down.'

Winnie picked up the watering can and watered her feet.

'Oo, that's nice!' she said, wiggling her steaming toes. 'I wish, I wish . . . Oo, I've got an idea!' said Winnie, and she pointed her wand at the watering can. '*Abracadabra!*' she shouted.

Instantly, there was a giant watering can up in the sky, spilling down a great showering waterfall of cold water.

'Lovely!' said Winnie, dancing in the shower. 'Come on, Wilbur!' But Wilbur was thrashing his wet tail and scowling at Winnie. 'Whoopsy warts,' said Winnie. 'I forgot that cats don't like water!'

II

'*Abracadabra!*'

In another instant the watering can was gone. Winnie stood there, dripping and steaming.

'I'm sorry, Wilbur. Sorry, sorry, sorry. Now, can we be friends again?'

Wilbur closed his eyes.

'I'll magic you a sun hat. I'll magic you some sunglasses!' said Winnie. '*Abracadabra Abracadabra!*'

Now Wilbur looked a dude, but he was still cross.

'This'll make you laugh!' said Winnie.
'What's brown and sticky and sounds like
a bell?'

Wilbur looked the other way and
pretended not to listen.

'Dung!' said Winnie. 'Dung's brown
and sticky and "dung" is the sound a big
bell makes! Get it?'

Wilbur just sniffed.

13

'I'll buy you a present, then. That'll
cheer you up,' said Winnie. She got her
broom.

'Jump up, Wilbur!'

Wilbur's ears flattened on his head,
but he climbed on board.

It was hot, flying.

'Let's go faster to make a breeze,' said
Winnie. '*Abracadabra!*'

In an instant, Wilbur had to cling on to
the broom with every claw. He lay flat and
he closed his eyes, his tail whizzing out
behind the broom.

14

'Wheeeee!' said Winnie. 'This is fun!'

'Mrrrow!' wailed Wilbur.

'Honestly! You just can't please some blooming cats!' said Winnie.

They got to the shops and parked the broom. But, 'Stop!' said Winnie. 'You wait in the broom basket, Wilbur, or you'll spoil your surprise.'

Wilbur was just climbing into the basket
when a little girl called Clara noticed him.

'Hello, Pussykins!' said Clara. 'Are you
hot, Pussykins? Are you hungry? Come
with me!' Clara hauled Wilbur out of the
basket. Wilbur was almost as big as Clara,
but Clara managed to carry and drag
Wilbur all the way to her house.

Clara's house was shady and cool.
Clara's fridge had cat food in it. Clara's
sisters all fussed over Wilbur and told him
what a very fine cat he was. Wilbur purred
so much that his whiskers sparked. Wilbur
was cool. Wilbur was being spoilt. Wilbur
was happy.

Winnie was feeling happier, too. As she
stepped into her favourite shop, a draught
of cool smelly air from a drain lifted her
hair and her dress and her spirits.

'Ooo!' giggled Winnie. 'This is lovely!'

18

Winnie looked at toad toasters and mouse mincers and maggot mashers and filth frothers and cockroach crushers and bat broilers before she found what she was after. She took her parcel back outside.

'Here I am, Wilbur!' said Winnie. 'Time to go home.'

19

Winnie picked up her broom and gave it a shake.

'Are you still sulking? Oh, stay in the basket if you want to.' Winnie hung her shopping from the front of the broom and climbed on board.

'Oooer!' said Winnie as the broom tipped forwards because of the weight of the parcel. 'You're heavy, Wilbur. And you'll get even heavier after you've used

the present I've bought you. Can you
guess what it is?' asked Winnie as the
broom rose into the air.

Wilbur said nothing.

'You mardy old mog!' said Winnie.
'Don't you want to know?'

Still nothing.

Winnie was getting hot again. She
was getting cross too. So she didn't say
anything else to Wilbur all the way home.

Winnie parked her broom.

'We're home! Out you get!'

Winnie lifted the lid of the basket.

'WILBUR!' wailed Winnie . . . for the
basket was empty.

Winnie felt empty too. Winnie felt
desperate.

'Oh, my Wilbur, I've left you behind!
Don't worry, Wilbur, I'm coming!'

Winnie jumped back onto her broom.

'Abracadabra!' she shouted.

Quick as a flash she shot through the sky, back to the shops. Winnie looked wildly all around.

'Where *is* he?' wailed Winnie.

'That black cat?' said a boy. 'Clara took him.'

'What?' whispered Winnie. 'He's been STOLEN?'

'They went that way,' said the boy.

Winnie waved her wand.

'*Abracadabra*, take me to Wilbur!' begged Winnie.

23

In an instant Winnie was inside Clara's house, landing on Clara's dad's lap.

'A witch!' he yelped, and he leapt up, dropping Winnie to the floor. And suddenly Winnie was face to face with a grinning, drooling face that she knew and loved well.

'Oh, Wilbur!' said Winnie.

'He's going to live with me for ever and ever,' said Clara. 'Aren't you, Pussykins?'

Wilbur was purring and dribbling and working his claws as six small hands brushed him and put hair-clips in his fur.

'But he's *my* friend!' said Winnie. 'Look, I bought him a present!'

It was the little girls who ripped open the present and found . . .

'An ice-cream machine!' said Winnie.
'Do you like it, Wilbur? I thought we
could make maggot-flavour ice cream with
flea sprinklies to cool us down.'

But Clara's mum had other ideas. She
made strawberry ice cream with hundreds
and thousands on top. Clara and her sisters
were suddenly more interested in ice cream
than in cats.

'Quick, let's go home,' whispered
Winnie.

Without the ice-cream machine, the
broom was balanced just right. Winnie
and Wilbur flew at normal speed, calmly
over the countryside, and it was nice.

They landed in Winnie's garden.

'What shall we do now?' asked Winnie.

Wilbur grinned and pointed at the
rhubarb patch. 'Prrrmeow,' he said.

'Good idea!' said Winnie.

Winnie and Wilbur lay under the shade
of a big rhubarb leaf, watching the sun
go down. Winnie held a stick with a bit
of string tied to it with a centipede on the
end which she waved up and down. As
she flicked the centipede upwards, the
toad on the leaf jumped for it, bouncing
the leaf under him. So the leaf fanned
Winnie and Wilbur till they were cool and
comfortable and kind to each other again.

'I've got another joke for you,' said
Winnie.

'Mrrow?'

'What's brown and sticky?'

Wilbur smiled. Wilbur pointed.

'Yes!' said Winnie. 'A stick is brown and sticky!'

WINNIE
Gets Cracking

When Winnie and Wilbur were queuing in the shop to buy their weekend sherbet bombs and gummy worms and liquorice rats' tails and pickled gherkins, they overheard Mrs Parmar, the school secretary, talking to the shopkeeper.

'I'll have a small box of cheap chocolates,' said Mrs Parmar.

'Special occasion, is it?' asked the shopkeeper.

'It's my birthday today,' said Mrs Parmar. *Sniff!* 'Not that anyone takes any notice of that. I can't afford much, but I do buy myself a little bit of chocolate each year. Nobody else will bother, and I do love chocolate.'

'That's as sad as a soggy guinea pig with no umbrella!' said Winnie, sticking her large nose in between Mrs Parmar and the shop man.

'Oh, it's you, is it, Winnie?' said Mrs
Parmar. 'I'm still trying to forget the times
you cooked and cleaned at the school!'
She clutched her box of chocolates and
backed away.

'Wilbur and me, we'll invite you for
a birthday tea!' said Winnie. 'You come
along to my house, Mrs Parmar, and
we'll give you a real treat!'

A weak wobbly smile spread over Mrs
Parmar's face. 'Well, I suppose that is
kind of you, but . . .'

'See you at four, then,' said Winnie. 'And there'll be a present as well as lots to eat!'

'Food?' said Mrs Parmar, looking into Winnie's shopping basket. 'Oh, dear!' And she fled from the shop.

Winnie and Wilbur went home and
began to plan.

'What can we give her for a present?'
said Winnie. 'She's a smart lady. Would she
like some of that nice haggis hand cream?'

'Mrrro!' Wilbur shook his head.

'Well, what about a big black bar of
squashed slug soap?' Wilbur shook his

36

head even harder. 'No? Something pretty, then. What about a cowpat paperweight? Or maggot earrings? No? Or . . . or . . . I've got it!' Winnie clapped her hands in excitement. 'Remember that story about some thingy or other that lays a golden egg every day? Well, if we could get one of those for Mrs Parmar she would soon get rich! She could buy chocolate every day!'

Wilbur grinned his agreement.

'What exactly was it that laid the golden egg, Wilbur?' wondered Winnie. 'What came before the egg?'

Wilbur shrugged.

'Whatever laid the egg must have come out of an egg, mustn't it?' Winnie scratched her head. 'And whatever it was that laid *that* egg must have come out of another egg. And whatever . . . Oh, I know what! *Abracadabra!*'

In an instant the floor was rolling with eggs: big eggs, small eggs, speckled eggs, plain eggs, white eggs, pink eggs, rough eggs, smooth eggs.

'Keep them warm, Wilbur!' said Winnie. So Wilbur spread his furry warmth over as many of the eggs as he could, while Winnie crouched and hugged around the rest. It wasn't long before—

Crack!

'Whoops!'

Crack!

'Meeow!'

Crack-crack-crack!

—the eggs began to hatch. Out of this egg came that. Out of that egg came this. And out of the other eggs came those.

40

'Aren't they sweet? But I'd better grow them up fast, so that they can lay their eggs in time for tea. **Abracadabra!** went Winnie.

And instantly the room was full of
flapping and clucking and squawking and
croaking and hissing. Then—**bump,
splat! Crash, squish!** There were
eggs being dropped all over the place.

'Can you see any golden ones, Wilbur?'
asked Winnie. 'Oh, blooming rhubarb,
what can we do with all these eggs?'

'Mrrow!' suggested Wilbur, miming
eating with a knife and fork.

'Clever you, Wilbur!' said Winnie. 'We'll
cook eggs for Mrs Parmar's birthday tea.
Now, shoo all this lot out into the garden,
will you, while I get cooking?'

With a hiss and a pounce, Wilbur soon
had them all flapping and slithering and
lumbering for the door and windows.

43

'Better get cracking!' said Winnie. She broke eggs and eggs and eggs and got whizzing with her mixer.

Winnie made woodlouse crunch soufflé. She made omelettes with toad tongue fillings. She made hard-boiled lizard egg and pondweed sandwiches.

'What a feast!' said Winnie. 'Set the table, Wilbur, it's nearly time. Put out proper napkins and everything because she's a very particular lady.'

44

Then Winnie stopped licking the mixing spoon as she remembered. 'Ooo, but we still haven't got her a present. And I *promised* her one! Oh, poor Mrs Parmar!'

'Ding-dong! Wiiiiinnnniiiieeee!' went the dooryell.

'It's her!'

Wilbur opened the door. There stood
a rather nervous looking Mrs Parmar in
her best dress.

'Come in!' said Winnie. 'Sit down!
We've made you a feast. There's even a
sponge cake with gherkin filling and lots
of candles. I wasn't sure how many
candles, so I just put on lots!' said Winnie.

'Oh!' said Mrs Parmar, looking at the table. 'I'm not *very* hungry, you know.'

'We might play some party games after, if you like!' said Winnie.

'I can't stay *very* long,' said Mrs Parmar, brushing some spiders off a chair and sitting down very carefully.

'Sandwich?' asked Winnie.

'Oh, those *do* look nice!' said Mrs Parmar in surprise. She took a sandwich and was about to bite into it when . . .

Clump-clump-clomp-plop!

A big brown creature walked across the
table, lifted its tail, and laid an egg on the
edge of Mrs Parmar's plate, catapulting the
lizard egg and pondweed sandwich—
splat—on to the far wall.

48

'Well, that *is* a surprise!' said Winnie,
rather embarrassed. 'I'm ever so sorry,
Mrs Parmar. I thought we'd got rid of all
the hatchings before you arrived.' Winnie
glared at Wilbur.

But Mrs Parmar had picked up the egg.
She looked at the egg. She sniffed the egg.
Then she nibbled the egg. And she smiled.

'Mrs Parmar?' said Winnie.

'This is wonderful!' said Mrs Parmar,
relaxing and laughing. 'I can't think of any
present I'd rather have than a freshly-laid
chocolate egg!'

'I did want you to have a golden one,'
said Winnie.

'But you can't eat golden eggs!' said
Mrs Parmar, taking another nibble. Wilbur
nodded his head to agree with such
wisdom, so rarely found
in people.

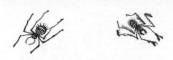

Mrs Parmar was too full of chocolate to eat anything else. But, once the tea was finished, they played 'Hunt the Chocolate Egg' because the chocodile had laid eggs all over the place.

'So many!' said Mrs Parmar. 'I can share them with the children at school. Then, perhaps, they might like me a little. That would be the best birthday present of all. Oh, thank you, Winnie!'

'You're welcome,' said Winnie. 'And you can take the chocodile as well, if you like.'

As she closed the door, Winnie said to Wilbur, 'Whoever would want chocolate, anyway, when they could have my trifle surprise?'

Broomstick
ALERT

'I'm bored!' said Winnie. 'I'm as bored as a snail is bored with the view inside its shell. I'm as bored as my toes are with the smell inside my socks. I'm as bored as . . .'

'Mrrow!' said Wilbur, and he put his paws over his ears.

'Am I being boring, Wilbur?' said Winnie.

'Mrrow!' said Wilbur crossly.

'What do people do to stop being bored?

Let's go down to the village and look in
the library,' said Winnie.

The library was full of bookshelves, and
full of people reading books.

'Look at them!' whispered Winnie. One
person was laughing. Another looked
frightened. 'How do books do that to
people?' asked Winnie. She took a book
from a shelf and looked at the black words
on a white page that she couldn't read.

Those marks didn't make her cry or laugh or feel anything. Winnie turned the book the other way up, but it didn't make any difference. Wilbur was lying on the carpet with a book open in front of him and he was cat-laughing.

'Mrow-ha-ha!'

'I want to know what's funny!' said Winnie. 'I'm blooming well going back to that school!'

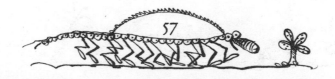

Winnie was in luck.

'Look at that, Wilbur! There's a whole flock of witches going to school today! And girls with plaits and stripy stockings and bears with suitcases and wizards with zigzags on their foreheads and . . . oh . . . almost everything except little ordinaries. They're as odd as a bag of ugly bug pick-n-mix. Come on, Wilbur, we'll fit in with the others today!'

'Who are you?' asked one small witch
in stripy tights.

'I'm Winnie the Witch,' said Winnie.

'So am I!' said the small one.

'Eh?' Winnie stood still and puzzled.

'How does that work, then?'

But Wilbur caught her cardigan in a
claw and hurried her into the classroom.

The teacher, in a red cloak with a hood,
was taking the register.

'Captain Teachum?'

'Here.'

'Professor Puffendorf?'

'Here.'

'Winnie the Witch?'

'Here,' said the little girl who
had talked to Winnie earlier.

'Here,' said Winnie.

'Who are you?' asked the teacher, glaring at Winnie. 'And what is that cat doing in my classroom? We don't allow witches in school!'

'But—!' began Winnie, looking around at lots of witches. But the teacher was pointing at the door.

'Out!' said the teacher. So Winnie and Wilbur went out of the classroom . . .

Oooff! and walked straight into Mrs Parmar, the school secretary. She was looking flustered.

'Oh, Winnie, I'm desperate!' said Mrs Parmar. 'Today is our Book Day and the dog ate all the storyteller's books, so he's not coming, and I've got children waiting for stories and nobody to tell them unless . . . oh, Winnie, could you do it? Pleeeeease?'

A smile like the crack in a boiled egg grew across Winnie's face. 'Yes!' she said.

So Mrs Parmar led Winnie and Wilbur
into the school library. Some children
were sitting on the carpet, looking up
at Winnie like vulture chicks in a nest
waiting to be fed.

'Now, children,' said Mrs Parmar.
'Winnie here is going to read to you.'

'Read?' said Winnie. 'I—' But Mrs
Parmar had already gone. 'Um,' said
Winnie. She took a book from the shelf.
'Look,' she said. 'A picture of a lion!'

'Read the story!' shouted the little extraordinaries.

'I can't!' said Winnie.

Gasp! went all the little extraordinaries.

'But,' said Winnie. 'I can make stories come out of books another way.' Winnie waved her wand. *'Abracadabra!'*

Instantly there was a great big, growly, toothy, prowly lion right inside the room! It was licking its lips and sniffing children and opening its big pink mouth wide to swallow a—

'Abracadabra!' shouted Winnie, and
instantly the lion was gone. 'Phew!' said
Winnie, feeling as weak as a worm. 'Er . . .
wasn't that fun?'

'No!' said the little extraordinaries.

'Oh. I'll do you a better one,' said
Winnie. She picked up a book with a
picture of a rocket on the cover.
'Who'd like to go into space?'

'Me, me, me, me, me, me, me, me!!!'

shouted all the little extraordinaries.

'Abracadabra!' went Winnie.

67

And, instantly, there was a rocket in the room. The rocket was so big that it stuck right through the school ceiling and you could see the sky above it. Wind blustered in through the hole, making wings flutter and witchy hair whirl.

'Wow!' said the little extraordinaries, gazing up at the huge rocket.

And out of the rocket stepped a big robot spaceman.

Gasp! went the little extraordinaries.

'Fly with me to Mars,' commanded the robot. 'Together, we will fight the dreaded Xargottlenaughts!'

'Ooo, yes, let's all go to Mars!' said Winnie. 'Put on your spacesuits, everyone! Get on board.'

68

Winnie was hopping on one leg, trying to pull on her spacesuit. She didn't notice Wilbur sneaking out of the door. But suddenly the door burst wide open.

'WHAT ON EARTH IS GOING ON?' boomed Mrs Parmar.

'Oh!' giggled Winnie. 'It almost wasn't "what on earth", Mrs Parmar. It was almost "what on Mars"!'

Mrs Parmar inflated like a balloon. She pointed at the robot.

'You! Out! Cover your ears, children!'

They all crouched and covered their ears as the robot shut himself into his rocket and fired the engines.

ROAR!

WHOOOOOSH!

70

Up shot the rocket, leaving a great hole
in the library ceiling.

'Um, that's the end of the story.
The end,' said Winnie. So the hole closed
and everything went back to normal in the
library.

Mrs Parmar told the children, 'Out you

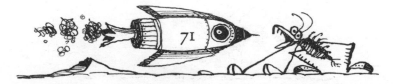

go and play.' Then she pointed at Winnie.
'You're fired!'

So Winnie and Wilbur went sadly out
to the bike shed to collect the broom.
They were just getting on board when
there was a shout from the playground.

'Help!'

A gust of wind had caught the wings
and capes of all the fairy and superhero
little extraordinaries, and they were rising
up into the sky and away from school!

'Help! Help!' they cried.

'I'm coming!' shouted Winnie.
'Hold tight, Wilbur!'

Up into the sky rose Winnie and
Wilbur on their broom. 'Grab hold
of Wilbur's paw!' Winnie told a fairy.
'Hold onto his tail!' she told a superhero.

And very soon Winnie had brought
them all safely back down to land.

'You saved the children, Winnie!'
said Mrs Parmar. 'You must come into
assembly so that the head teacher can
thank you properly.'

In assembly little Winnie the Witch
won the fancy dress prize. Big Winnie
the Witch won a medal for being a hero.

'You know what, Wilbur?' said Winnie as they walked happily home. 'There are more kinds of magic than *Abracadabra* magic.'

'Mrrow?' asked Wilbur.

'I think stories are magic too,' said Winnie.

'Purrrr,' agreed Wilbur.

Whizz-Bang
WINNIE

'Ooo, look at that! Fancy hanging your
washing all over the street!' said Winnie
as she and Wilbur flew over the village.
'Ooo, no! It's not knickers and socks,
it's flags and bunting! There must be
something going on in the village. Hold
tight, Wilbur, let's go and find out what!'

They landed beside a man on a ladder,
tying up the bunting. *Whoops!* He
wobbled when he saw them.

'I didn't scare you, did I?' said Winnie. 'What's going on?'

'Big race, this afternoon,' said the man.

'What sort of a race?' asked Winnie.

'Proper one,' said the man, tying the last knot of the bunting string to the lamp post, and climbing down his ladder. 'Drivers in helmets and zip-up suits. Low down cars with big fat wheels that squeal and smoke when they go round corners.'

The man rubbed his hands together and
smiled happily. 'It'll be a really proper
race. Lots of noise. A few crashes.
Tea afterwards.'

'What sort of noise?' asked Winnie.

'**Brrrrrrroooooom** sorts of noise!'
said the man.

'Oh, I've got a broom!' said Winnie,
waving her broom at the man.

The man laughed. 'That's a woman's kind of a broom, that is. That's a broom for cleaning, not for racing!'

'I could race you on this broom and beat you any day of the week!' said Winnie.

'Mrrow!' agreed Wilbur, flying a paw fast past the man's eyes to show him what Winnie's broom could do.

'Well,' said the man, 'if you take my advice, darling, you'll keep that broom in the kitchen and leave racing to the men and the machines.'

'Huh!' said Winnie. 'I'll see you this afternoon!'

The man shook his head. 'You can't go in for the race if your vehicle hasn't got wheels.' He pointed to a poster.

Hot wheels race! Open to all comers.
Sponsored by Tyres That Never Tire.

'No, love. You'd do best to help out
with serving the teas. I'm sure the ladies could
lend you a pinny.'

'I'll not be serving teas! I'll be serving you
right, that's what I'll be serving!' said Winnie.

'Hadn't you better get back to hanging up your washing, mister? There's nothing to stop a broom having wheels, is there? Let's go on a wheel hunt.'

'Mrrow!' said Wilbur.

They looked in there. She looked under that. He looked inside those.

And they found wheels like this . . .
and this . . . and these . . . and those.

'Hand me the hammer, Wilbur,' said
Winnie. Then she began **bang-bang-
banging** the wheels onto her broom.

'There, Wilbur! Isn't that the best
wheelie broom you've ever seen? Hop on,
you can try it out, Wilbur!'

Wilbur's knees were knocking. Wilbur's ears were flat on his head.

'Put on your helmet.' Winnie rammed a bucket onto Wilbur's head.

'Hold tight!' said Winnie. Wilbur closed his eyes. He clung tight with his claws.

'Abracadabra!' shouted Winnie, waving her wand to make the broom go fast. Instantly rocket fire flared from the broom's bristles, and the broom shot

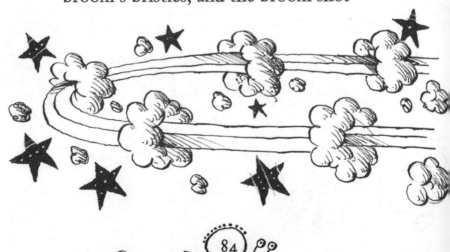

forward . . . and round in a circle. Round and round and round and round so fast it was just a blur of stick and twigs and fire and frightened cat.

'Oh, botherarmarations!' said Winnie. 'We'll never win the race like that!'

'Mrrrrrroooooowwwww!' wailed Wilbur.

'Oh, poor Wilbur!' said Winnie, snatching up her wand. *'Abracadabra!'*

Instantly the broom stopped still.
But Wilbur didn't. He shot forward
and landed, with his head still spinning
round and round and round.

Winnie tried again. **Bang! Bang!
Bang!** 'Ouch, ouch ouch! Blooming
botherarmarations and fleas' fingernails,
I've banged my thumb!'

Winnie fixed the wheels again: this time
with bigger wheels at the back and smaller
wheels at the front.

'Hop on, we'll try again,' said Winnie.

'Mrrow!' Wilbur tried to run, but
Winnie caught him by the tail and plonked
him on the broom. 'Don't worry, I'm
coming with you this time! And I'm not
going to magic it fast.'

Winnie pulled the broom to the top of the hill. She sat on it, then pushed off . . . **w h e e - h u p - b u m p - d o w n** — 'Mrrow!' — **w h e e - h u p - b u m p - down** — 'Yeouch!' — **whee-hup** —

'Stop!' shouted Winnie, but the broom didn't stop. It went faster, and the **hup-bump** got faster too. 'Where's my wand?' screeched Winnie. *'Abra* — !' But Winnie's wand caught in one of the spokes of the wheels.

Lurch-skid-clatter-bang!

88

'Ouch!'

'Meowch!'

Bumped and bruised and banged and biffed, they got to their feet and looked at the scatter of wheels and the broken broom.

'We won't win any races on that!' said Winnie.

Just then they heard the loudspeakers down in the village announcing the race.

'It's about to start!' said Winnie. 'Come on, Wilbur! Even if we can't go in for the race, we can watch it! How are we going to get down there fast? I know . . . *Abracadabra!*'

In an instant, Winnie had roller skates on her feet. **Crash!** The next instant she'd fallen.

'Ouch!'

Holding on to Wilbur and rubbing her bottom, Winnie wobbled upright.

'You too, Wilbur!' she said.

'Abracadabra!'

Splat! Wilbur instantly had castors under each paw, and those castors had gone in different directions. Out went his legs. Down went Wilbur.

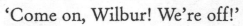

'Mrrow!'

'Come on, Wilbur! We're off!'

Winnie and Wilbur wobbled, then
strode, getting a little braver all the time.
Soon Winnie was bent over, one hand
behind her back, the other arm swinging
to speed her faster as she swished along
like a champion. There was a sound of
engines revving.

'Weeeeeee! Speeeeedy meeeee!' went
Winnie.

With a great roar, the cars were off and
racing!

'Come on, Wilbur!'

Wilbur copied Winnie's skating style
and managed to stay on his paws.

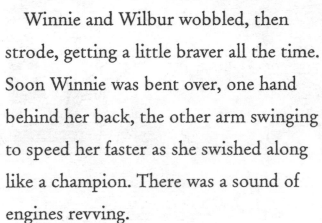

They got to the hill that ran down into
the village just as the cars came around the
corner.

'Weeeeee Ooooooo, Wilbuuuuuuurrr,
this is a bit toooooo faaaaaast!'

'Mrrrow!' wailed Wilbur. Faster and
faster they shot onto the road, whizzing
past roaring cars. They were going a bit
too fast.

'Wiiiilllllbbbbuuuurrrrr!' shouted
Winnie. 'How do I make the skates stop?'

But Wilbur didn't know either.
'Mmmeeeeeeooooowwwww!'

And suddenly both of them were
tripped and tangled in tape.

'HOORAY!' shouted the crowd.

'Why are they cheering?' said Winnie.
'I've never had so many bruises in my life!'

'They're cheering because you won the race, missus!' said big Jerry from next door, stepping out of the crowd. 'Shall I carry you and Wilbur home?'

96

'That would be lovely,' said Winnie.
'I'll make us all a nice cup of garlic
blossom and ditchwater tea. Then it
will have been a proper race, with lots of
noise, a few crashes, and tea afterwards.'

'Lovely!' said Jerry.

WINNIE

and the Toof Fairy

Winnie and Wilbur were watching a
wrestling match on telly and sharing a
few snacks.

'Pull him over!' shouted Winnie at the
telly. She jumped up from the sofa. 'Go on,
grab him!' She shot out an arm to grab the
air to show the wrestler how he should be
doing it, but unfortunately Wilbur was in
the way. **POW!**

'Mrrow!'

Wilbur's paw was over his mouth.
There was a look of panic in his eyes.

'Oh, heck, Wilbur!' said Winnie. 'Have
I punched all your teeth out?'

Wilbur slowly took his paws away from
his mouth. He opened his mouth and felt
for each tooth with his tongue. They were
all still there.

'Thank stinky cheese for that!' said
Winnie. 'Shall I take you to Mr Drillikins
the dentist, just to check you over?'

'Mrow-ow-ow!' said Wilbur, hurrying
up the curtains to get out of reach.

'All right, all right!' said Winnie. 'But you be careful. Those teeth might be loose. You suck a nice warm-worm and frogspawn smoothie through a straw. I'll finish off the nibbles by myself.'

Winnie settled back on the sofa.

'Trip him up! Pull his hair!' she shouted while she dipped an elephant's toenail into stinkwort sauce and popped it into her mouth. Chew-chew. 'Tickle him!' she screamed as she took a liquorice rat's tail and began to chew-chew-chew on that.

But, suddenly, 'Mnnn!' mumbled Winnie, her hand to her mouth. She stuck long fingers into her mouth and pulled out . . .

'A toof!'

'Meeow!' said Wilbur, looking with interest.

'What am I going to do without thith toof?' asked Winnie, holding it up. 'I need thith toof! I can't talk properly wivout it! I'll look like one of them wrethlerth on the telly! I'll never be beautiful again! And I'll thtarve to death. What'th that?'

Wilbur was nudging Winnie, offering her his straw.

'No!' wailed Winnie. 'I don't want thmoothies thucked through a thtraw!' But Wilbur had grabbed hold of the telephone book and was pointing at a phone number. 'NO, no, no!' wailed Winnie, even louder. 'I'm not going to Mr Drillikinth! Never!'

But Wilbur had one more helpful hint to try. He was pirouetting on his toes, his arms curved above his head and a soppy look on his face.

'What on erf?' asked Winnie. Then she got it. 'Oh, I know! You're being a fairy!' Wilbur nodded enthusiastically. 'Of courth!' said Winnie. 'I can leave my toof for the toof fairy and get a wifth from her in ecthchange for the toof. Oooo, what thall I chooth for my wifth, Wilbur?'

Actually, choosing her wish was easy. There was one thing more than any other that Winnie wanted just then.

'I mutht write a note to tell the fairy my wifth,' said Winnie. 'Where'th my pen, Wilbur?'

Winnie scrawled with her pen.

'There! Lookth good, doethn't it!'

Wilbur curled a lip and shook his head.

'Oh, thtop looking at me like that, cat!'
said Winnie. 'You know I'm not very good
at writing. I jutht thought a fairy might
underthtand. Will you write it for me,
pleathe, Wilbur?'

Wilbur did write it, in his best paw-writing. He wrote it very tiny and just right for a fairy. It said:

Please give Winnie
a new tooth.
Thank you.
W & W

'Thweet dreamth, Wilbur,' said Winnie.

Winnie was woken in the night by
something tickling around her face.

'Atithoo!' sneezed Winnie. Then, 'Poo!'
she shouted. 'What'th that 'orrible
thmell?' Then she sank back into snoring,
Snooore, phiew, snooore, phiew.

The little-wittle tooth fairy smelt of summer breezes wafting over dew-fresh meadow flowers sprinkled with icing sugar and love. Nobody had ever said 'poo' to her before. She put her tiny fists on her teeny pink waist. She stomped weeny green-slippered feet across Winnie's pillow.

She grabbed hold of a titchy handful of
Winnie's tangle of hair, and heaved herself
up onto Winnie's cheesy-white cheek.
Then she took her wincy little wand and—
WHACK!—she walloped it hard onto
Winnie's great snoring mountain of a nose.

'Eh? What?' said Winnie, sitting up.

The fairy tumbled, but she flapped her incy-wincy mauve wings to flutter to where the tooth and the note were waiting for her.

The tooth fairy held her meeny-miny-mo wand to glow over the note, and she read Winnie's wish. And a minuscule wicked grin came on to her fairy face. **Zip-zap** went the wincy yellow wand and—

Gulp! 'Eh, what was that?' said Winnie, feeling for her mouth. 'Hey, Wilbur! Guess what? I've got my new tooth! I can say, "Six silly slugs sat sipping sausage syrup through straws!" My wish has come true! Here, let me have a look!'

Winnie jumped out of bed and grabbed her wand.

'Abracadabra!'

Instantly the candles were lit and a mirror was gleaming with a come-hither look. Winnie arranged herself into a charming pose in front of the mirror. Then she smiled, and . . . oh, dear.

'Mrrow-hissss!' Wilbur scrabbled under the bed covers.

'Oh, heck!' cried Winnie as she saw

herself. 'Whatever has that blooming fairy
done? She's given me a fearful fang! I look
a right fright!'

Winnie's eyes were darting here and there, looking for a fairy twinkle . . . and she spotted it, still on her pillow.

'There it is!' shouted Winnie. She swung her wand to swat it, *'Abracadabra!'*

Instantly the twinkle around the fairy was replaced by a buzz of midges around the fairy.

But . . . **zip-zap** went the tiddly
tooth fairy wand. And instantly Winnie
was covered in warts.

'Abracadabra!'
The fairy smelt of manure.
Zip-zap!
Winnie's skin turned blue.
'Abra—'

'MMEEEEOOWWW!' interrupted Wilbur. He'd poked his head out from the covers and found something nestling under the pillow. It was something as tall as the tooth fairy and not perhaps quite as white as it might be, but Wilbur knew just what it was and where it was needed. He held it out to Winnie.

'My tooth!' said Winnie. 'My very own dear tooth! Oh, *Abracadabra!*'

And instantly Winnie's own tooth was back in her head, and the fang and the warts and blue had all gone. And so had the tooth fairy.

'Well,' said Winnie as she snuggled back into bed. 'That just goes to show, doesn't it?'

'Meow?' asked Wilbur.

'It shows that if you want a wish doing, you'd better just blooming well do the wish yourself,' said Winnie.

'Meeow,' agreed Wilbur.

Itchy
WITCHY

Winnie held the telling-moan away from her ear and winced at big sister Wanda's voice.

'Are you listening, Winnie?' screeched Wanda. 'The witches' cat show is tomorrow. I'm putting Wayne in for it, of course. He won it last year, you know. I've just had his teeth whitened. And highlights put in his fur.'

Wayne was Wanda's snooty sleek-as-a-panther cat.

'Have you still got that scraggy old catty thing of yours?' asked Wanda. 'What was he called?'

'He's called Wilbur,' said Winnie. 'And he's lovely.'

'Well, we'll all see just how lovely he is at the show, won't we! He hee!' laughed Wanda.

'No,' said Winnie. 'I wasn't going to—'

'He hee! He hee!' cackled Wanda. 'I knew it! I said to Wayne, I said, "I bet Winnie won't dare to put that Wilbur in for the show because she knows very well he'll come bottom of the whole thing!" He heee! I just knew it!'

Winnie glared at the telling-moan. 'Well, you knew wrong, Wanda the Witch!' she said. 'The only bottom thing at the show will be your Wayne winning the competition for the cat who has the witch with the biggest bottom—YOURS! Wilbur *will* be in the show, and he might just win it! So there!'

Winnie slammed down the telling-moan. Then she chewed a nail. 'Oh, banana bandages!' she said to herself. 'Winnie the Witch, whatever have you gone and done now?'

Winnie looked at Wilbur lying happily in the sun. There was a spider's web stuck between Wilbur's ears. There was a bald patch on his back where he'd rolled around  on hot tar and it had pulled some of his fur off. There was some pond slime hanging from his tail. And flies were hovering over him in a way that suggested that he might not be smelling very fresh at the moment.

Winnie found a pair of shark-fin scissors, some carpet shampoo, a big bottle of skunk scent, a brush, a comb, some slug-slime hair gel, some gizzard glue and a ball of black wool, and she took them all outside.

'Oh, Wilbur!' she called.

Wilbur opened one eye.

'Come to Winnie, Wilbur!' called Winnie.

Wilbur's ears went flat onto his head. Up he leapt, and he was about to run when—

'**Abracadabra!**' went Winnie, and instantly poor Wilbur was frozen still. 'I'm sorry about this, Wilbur, but I've got to make you beautiful,' said Winnie.

Winnie got to work, washing . . . and combing . . . and sticking wool over bald bits. And then she saw a little something **hop-hop-HOP** in Wilbur's fur.

'Oh, heck, Wilbur, you've got fleas!'
said Winnie. She caught the flea mid-hop
and popped it into her mouth. 'Mmm,'
she said. 'Quite tasty in a tickle-your-
taste-buds kind of way, but I don't think
they give you a prize at the show if you've
got fleas. Come on, Wilbur. We're off to
the vet's to get you some flea treatment,'
said Winnie.

Winnie un-froze Wilbur once he was
inside the carrying box. It's horrible being
in a box. There's nowhere to hide. Wilbur
felt the jolting and swaying as Winnie got
off her broomstick and carried the box
into the surgery. Then he smelt that vetty
smell.

'Meeeeooooowww!' he wailed miserably.

'My goodness,' said the vet. 'When did this animal last see a vet?'

'Oh, ages ago,' said Winnie. 'He hates vets.'

'Mrrrow!' went Wilbur, then he showed just how much he hated vets by scrabbling up this one and sitting on his head. He took off the vet's toupee when Winnie lifted him down.

'Is that an animal that went up and died there?' asked Winnie.

The vet squirted stuff on to Wilbur to
get rid of the fleas. The fleas march-
hopped—cough, sneeze!—down off
Wilbur and on to Winnie and the vet.
Itch-itch, scratch.

'Now,' said the vet. Itch, scratch.
'This cat needs injections for cat flu and
cat cold and cat sore-throat and cat
ingrowing toenails and cat tennis elbow.'

'Are you sure?' said Winnie. 'How much will that lot cost?'

'Let me see,' said the vet, and he began poking numbers into his calculator. **Itch, scratch.** Winnie saw a number getting longer and longer.

'Quick, Wilbur!' she whispered. 'Let's go!'

Wilbur did look very smart at the show, even if he didn't look happy. Winnie felt worried and **itch-itch** scratchy.

But Wanda and Wayne were smug-as-a-bug happy. Wayne lounged in a suave and sophisticated smiley way.

'What do you think of my Wayne, then,
Winnie? Just feel how silky his fur is. Go
on, Win, have a feel!' said Wanda.

So Winnie reached out a hand to feel how
soft Wayne was. And as she touched him . . .
this hopped . . . and that hopped . . . and
those hopped . . . off Winnie and on to
Wayne. **Itch-itch, scratch. Itch-
itch-itch, scritchety-scratch.**

'Oo, here comes the judge!' said Wanda.

137

'Just watch what he says about Wayne and Wilbur, he hee!' **Itch-scratch,** went Wayne. 'Don't do that, Wayne darling,' said Wanda. 'Be nice for the judge.'

The judge poked at Wilbur first.

'Mrrrow!' went Wilbur. He'd had enough of being poked for one day.

The judge lifted Wilbur's tail.

'Hisss!' Scratch! went Wilbur.

'Disqualified!' said the judge.

'He heee!' said Wanda.

The judge poked at Wayne.

'Purrrr!' went Wayne.

The judge lifted Wayne's tail.

'Purrr!' Smarm! went Wayne.

'Very nice indeed,' said the judge.

139

But just then—**itch**, went Wayne.
Itch-itch, scratch-scratch. And
then the judge felt an itch and began to
scratch.

'Uh!' he shouted, snatching his hands
away from Wayne. 'This cat has got
FLEAS!'

He was about to disqualify Wayne, but there was no need to because everybody was disqualifying themselves, running and shoving to get away from the fleas and the show.

'What a lot of fuss over a few fleas!' said Winnie, happily scratching herself. 'Call themselves witches! Huh! Come on, let's go home, Wilbur.'

Back home Wilbur rolled in the grass to get himself back to himself.

'Here's a rosette for you!' said Winnie, and she fixed a dried tarantula to his ear. 'It's for being the best cat for me!'

'Purrr!' said Wilbur proudly.

They sat and ate squashed-flea biscuits. And all the fleas that had fled to Winnie's head, hopped back on to Wilbur because Wilbur tasted nicer, if you were a flea.

And so all the fleas were back home, too.
Except for one adventurous flea who had
hopped on to Wayne and then on to Wanda
because he liked the taste of her hair spray.
So Wanda was going **itch-itch,
scritchety-scratch.**

Hee heee!

WINNIE'S
One-Witch Band

Winnie was just pegging out her
washing when she heard music coming
from the village. Winnie stopped still,
a pair of bloomers held up in the air, and
she listened.

'Who can it be?' Winnie asked Wilbur.
'It sounds the way my tummy sounds after
I've eaten one of your snake sausage and
chilli stews then drunk a fizz-pop pond
cordial sucked through a straw,' said Winnie.

145

'Except that this sound is less gurgly. Let's go and find out where it's coming from!'

So Winnie and Wilbur went down into the village, and they found the sound coming from the library.

'They're all singing!' said Winnie, as she peeped through the window.

'La la laaa!' warbled the ladies' high-up voices. 'Bom boom-boom-bum,' sang the low-down men's voices. 'Traliddle-traloddle,' they all sang together. 'Tra . . .

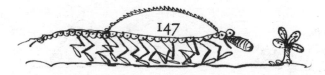

AHHHH!' they shrieked as they suddenly
saw Winnie's and Wilbur's faces squashed
against the glass.

'Why ever have they stopped?' asked
Winnie. She soon found out why.

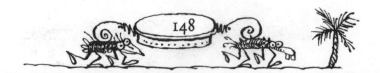

The conductor came to the library door.

'Go away!' he said. 'You're frightening my choir and spoiling my rehearsal! We have a concert to prepare!'

'What concert?' asked Winnie.

'The library concert,' said the conductor. 'To raise money to buy more books for the library.'

'And who's in the choir?' asked Winnie.

'Anybody who wants to sing,' said the conductor.

'Ooooo, goody-goody!' said Winnie, pushing her way into the library. 'Where do I stand?'

'Well,' said the conductor, looking worried. 'Um . . . what kind of voice do you have?'

'A good loud one!' said Winnie.

'No, no,' said the conductor, flapping his hands like a baby bird. 'What I meant was, do you have a low voice or a high voice?'

'Oh, I can go up and down like a kangaroo in a lift!' said Winnie.

'Perhaps I'd better try you out,' said the conductor wearily. He sat down at a piano and played—**plink-plonk-plink-plonk-plink-plonk-plink**—up and down. 'Now, sing that back to me, please,' he told Winnie.

Winnie opened her mouth and—

croak-moan-honk-screechety-croak—down and up, sang Winnie.

Wilbur had his paws over his ears. The choir winced. The conductor had gone pale. 'Er . . . ' he said. 'I don't think we can use you in our choir, Winnie.'

'Why not?' asked Winnie. 'Wasn't I loud enough? I can go louder. Listen!'

CROAK-MOAN-HONK-SCREECHETY-CROAK!

Books fell from the shelves all around. The flowers in the vase wilted. Mice ran for their holes. Bookworms buried themselves deep into the fattest volumes they could find. And the choir all fainted—**thunk!**

153

'Er . . . no,' said the conductor weakly holding on to a bookcase. 'I'm afraid that really wasn't good enough.'

'Oh,' said Winnie. 'So you don't want me?'

The conductor shook his head.

There was silence for a moment, then . . . 'Ooo, but I've got a good idea!' said Winnie. 'My cat, Wilbur, he's got a lovely voice. You listen to him!'

'Must I?' said the conductor.

'Go on, Wilbur!' said Winnie.

Wilbur looked bashful. His toes turned in, he looked at the floor with a silly grin on his face, and shook his head.

'Go ON, Wilbur!' urged Winnie.

Wilbur meow-giggled.

But then he sat up straight and opened
his mouth and everyone in the choir
covered their ears.

But what came out of Wilbur's
mouth was beautiful. 'Meeeeoow! Mew-
mew-mew, miow-wow!'

As Wilbur sang, the choir took their
hands from their ears and joined in.

'Oh!' said the conductor, clasping his
hands together. 'Oh, Wilbur, that was
dee-vine!' Then the conductor frowned.
'But won't it look rather odd if we have a
cat in our choir?'

156

'Oh-oh, I know what we can do!' said
Winnie, jumping around in excitement.

'If I wear a long skirt, then Wilbur can
hide under it and sing and I'll just open and
close my mouth and everybody will think
it's me who is singing. It'll look quite
normal! I'll show you how. Sing, Wilbur!'

157

Wilbur sang—'Meeeeoow! Mew-mew-
mew, miow-wow!'—while Winnie silently
opened and closed her mouth and waggled
her eyebrows. She waved her hands
expressively, knocking the few books left
on shelves—**thump thumpety-
thump**—onto the floor.

'Good, wasn't it?' said Winnie, when they'd
finished. 'Shall I go and find a long skirt?'

'Er . . . no,' said the conductor. 'I have a better solution! Wilbur can be our soloist! He can perform *with* the choir while not being part *of* the choir. Would that suit you, Wilbur? Do you have your own bow tie?'

Giggle, went Wilbur. 'Meow.' And he put a paw to his mouth and pretended to be embarrassed.

'Show off!' said Winnie.

The conductor pointed his baton at Winnie. 'You had better go!'

So Winnie went, stamping her feet crossly

stomp-stomp

like a drum—out of the library. She went

home and cooked herself some tea

crash! bang! clang!

went the pots and pans,

sounding like cymbals.

Winnie took her tea out into the garden.

Tweet-tweet,

like a pipe, went a little bird.

Hoot,

like an organ, went an owl.

Winnie stopped eating and listened.

Croak-croak-belch,

like no musical instrument

ever invented, went a toad.

'That has given me a brillaramaroodle

idea!' said Winnie suddenly. 'Where's my

wand, Wilbur?' But Wilbur wasn't there.

'Oh, I'll get it myself,' said Winnie.

Then she waved it, *'Abracadabra!'*

In an instant, Winnie was outside the
library, covered in sounds. She had
hooting owls of different sizes on her
shoulders and head. She had a toad in her
pocket which could be squeezed for a
croak. She had a rat in another pocket
with a tail hanging out to be pulled when
she wanted a squeal. She had saucepan-lid
cymbals strapped to her knees, and
clackety clogs on her feet.

'I'm a one-witch band!' she said, and
the wand conducted, all on its own.

**Crash-clang-croak-squeak,
hoot-hoot-hoot-hoot-ping!**

That last ping wasn't really part of the
music. It was the elastic going on Winnie's
knickers.

Inside the library, Wilbur and the choir were performing to people who had bought tickets.

'Meeeoww! Tra-la-la-la-la, boom-boom-boom!'

Outside the library, Winnie played while the children gathered to hear and cheer her. And when the choir concert finished, Wilbur came outside and joined Winnie.

'*Abracadabra!*'

Instantly, Wilbur had clogs on his paws, and all the right moves. Wilbur tap-danced to Winnie's band. He held out her hat and collected lots more money for the library. And everybody danced.

164

As they—**clank-crash-croak tappety-tap-parp-whoops!**—walked home in the moonlight, Winnie said to Wilbur, 'Life is a kind of music, when you think about it.'

'Meeow,' agreed Wilbur happily.

165

WINNIE
Says Cheese

'Oo, look at little you with your pink nose and fluffy-wuffy coat!' said Winnie, showing Wilbur a photo in an album. 'You were such a sweet 'ickle kitten in those days!'

Wilbur smiled and rubbed his face against Winnie. He gazed up at her. 'Purrr!'

Winnie had a soppy look on her face. 'Do you know,' she said, 'I remember the day I chose teeny little Wilbur out of all

those little fluff-ball kittens in the cave. I chose you instead of any of those others because . . .' Winnie's face changed. 'Oh, yes, you dug your claws into my cardigan and you wouldn't let go and the goblin grabbed my broom and wouldn't give it back until I paid for you and promised to take you away.'

'Mrrow!'

'Oh, but you were as cute as a newt in those days, Wilbur!' Winnie sniffed. 'Of course you've grown big and shaggy and smelly since then.' Winnie looked at the wet patch on her sleeve where Wilbur had drooled. 'And a bit disgusting, if you don't mind me saying so, Wilbur.'

169

Wilbur did mind her saying so. Wilbur turned the pages of the album until he came to some photos of Winnie when she was a titchy little witchy girl. Wilbur nudged Winnie to show that he thought that she was sweet when she was little too. And she was. Little Winifred Witch had gappy teeth in a plump face and lots of frizzy black hair.

'Ah!' said Winnie. But Wilbur hadn't finished. He kept turning the pages, and Winnie saw herself growing older and stringier and tattier and more wrinkly with each one.

'Oh, where's my wand, Wilbur?' shouted Winnie. 'I can soon sort this.' She pointed the wand at her face. *'Abracadabra!'* She pointed it at her hair. *'Abracadabra!'*

171

The next instant Winnie didn't look like Winnie any more. Winnie fingered her face and her hair.

'It feels funny,' she said. She could hardly move her mouth because her skin was so tight. 'It's as smooth and soft as an eel's eyeball. Am I beautiful, Wilbur?'

'Hisss!'

'Let's have a look see,' said Winnie, and she marched over to the mirror in the hall.

'AAAAH! Ooo, no!' said Winnie, clutching her face. 'It's Mask Woman! That's not me! Ooo, quick, get me back to being real, even if real does mean wrinkles! *Abracadabra!*'

And real Winnie was back again, but still frowning at the mirror. 'Mouldy maggots, I've just realized something!' she said. 'Look at that!'

Winnie grabbed a photo. 'Mildewed midges, Wilbur! I'm wearing exactly the same outfit now as I was then, and that photo was taken umpteen years ago! It's time I changed what I wear, even if I don't change me! I want some smart new photos for the album.'

So Winnie looked for witch clothes on the internet.

'I'll have one of those!' said Winnie. 'Ooo, and them in the orange with silver trimmings! And I'd look a treat in that one!'

Click, click went Winnie, then she scowled. 'What size am I, Wilbur? Oh, heck, I can't be doing with all this. Pass my wand over!' Winnie zapped the computer screen with her wand. *'Abracadabra!'*

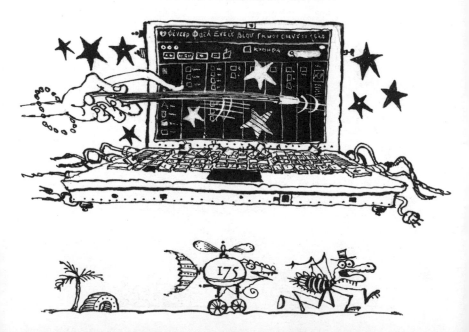

Instantly there appeared one of these . . .
and two of those . . . and some of them . . .

'I'm going to try them all on!' said
Winnie.

Winnie stripped down. She pulled on the
hot pants.

Wilbur sniggered into a paw.

'My legs look like twiglets!' said Winnie.
'What would cover them up?'

Winnie pulled the ball gown over her
head and let it cascade down her.

'Oo, this feels as gorgeous as a trifle
surprise with creamed worm topping!'

Wilbur spun his paw, so Winnie did a
twirl to make the skirt stick out. But she
twirled a bit too fast.

'Oooer, I've come over all dizzy!'

CRASH!

Winnie fell on her bum, her twiglet legs in the air.

'Did I look like Cinderella?' Winnie asked Wilbur as she got herself up. Wilbur made a face. 'More like an ugly sister, I suppose,' said Winnie. 'Botherarmarations. Nothing really suits, does it?'

Winnie put her fists to her skinny hips. 'I wish I was like you, Wilbur,' she said. 'You wear the same old black fur every blooming day, and it somehow looks just right.' Then Winnie brightened. 'Hey, that's a thought, Wilbur! Why don't I try black fur like yours?' Winnie snatched up her wand, just as there was a thumping at the front door. '*Abracadabra!*' shouted Winnie.

178

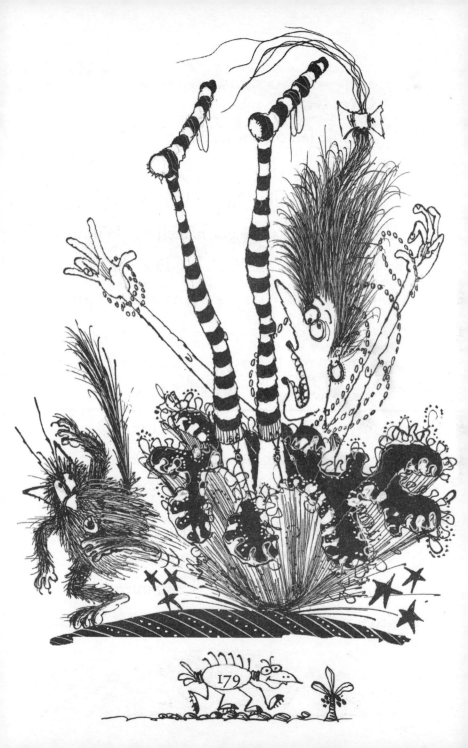

Instantly, there was Winnie, dressed top to toe in a kind of black furry hooded Babygro with added ears and a tail.

'Lovely and warm!' said Winnie, admiring and stroking herself in the mirror and giving her tail a twirl before she hurried to answer the door.

Thump, screech, creeeeak!

Winnie opened the door and . . .

'Wooof woof woof yap-yappety yap!'

Wilbur watched in amazement as
Winnie shot back into the house, closely
followed by the dog from next door that
was snip-snapping at her tail.

'Wilbur, HEEEELLLLPPPP!'
shouted Winnie.

'Scruff!' called the voice of Jerry, Winnie's giant neighbour. 'Bad boy, come back, Scruff!' Jerry folded himself over at the waist so that he could fit into Winnie's house. 'I'm ever so sorry about him, missus!' said Jerry. 'Scruff!'

Winnie had clambered on to the top of the dresser and was balanced there, but the dresser was swaying. The plates on it were swaying too.

'Grrrrr!' said Scruff.

'He don't know who you are, looking like that, missus! He's only being a good guard dog,' said Jerry.

'Well, I don't want to be blooming guarded!' said Winnie, grasping her tail to get it out of dog-teeth reach.

Jerry scratched his head. 'Why are you dressed like that, missus, if you don't mind me asking?'

'Grrrr-yap!' Scruff jumped up, his paws on the dresser.

'Oooer!' wailed Winnie as the dresser began to tip in slow motion, plates falling and smashing one by one. Winnie was falling too. 'Because . . .' **Smash!** 'I wanted . . .' **Smash!** 'to look . . .' **Smash-smash!** 'DIFFERENT!' **Smash-smash-smash!**

Winnie landed in the pile of broken crockery. For a moment there was stillness and silence.

Then Winnie pushed back her hood.

'YAP-ya—oh!' said Scruff, and his tail
went between his legs.

Winnie sat amongst the mess, but
suddenly she smiled. Then she cackled
with laughter.

CACKLE CACKLE CACKLE CACKLE CACKLE CACKLE

'Well, I suppose I do look different, don't I? Fetch the camera, Wilbur! Cheddar-Lancashire-Red Leicester-Wymeswold-Stilton . . . hurry up, Wilbur! . . . Double Gloucester-Stinking Bishop-Cheshire-Wensleydale-CHEESE!'

Click! went Wilbur.

'Your turn now!' said Winnie. So Wilbur stuck Winnie's hat on his head, and grinned his best grin.

'Mrreee-ow!'

Click! went Winnie. Then **Click!**
Click! because Jerry's and Scruff's faces
looked so funny and she wanted them in the
album too. 'There,' she said. 'Plenty of new
photos, and every one of them as daft as a
knotted noodle. Now, what shall we do?'

'Play frisbee?' suggested Jerry.

'With all these cracked plates!' said
Winnie. 'Good idea!'

So they went and played in the garden,
and had a smashing time.

WINNIE'S
Awful Auntie

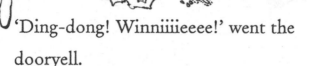

'Ding-dong! Winniiiieeee!' went the dooryell.

'What? Who? Where am I?' Winnie sat up in bed, suddenly awake. 'Did you hear something, Wilbur?'

Wilbur rolled over, stretched, yawned, and flopped back into sleep.

'Just a dream then,' said Winnie. She lay down, stretched, yawned and . . .

'Wiiiinnnniiiiieeee!' went the dooryell.

'Oh, nits' knickers, there really is somebody there,' muttered Winnie. 'I'd better have a look.'

Winnie went to the window and peeped out. 'Oh, gnats' kneecaps, it's Auntie Aggie. Look at all that luggage! She's planning to stay!'

Wilbur buried his head under the sheets.

'It's no good hiding,' said Winnie. 'She always knows.' Winnie called out of the window, 'I'll be down in the shake of a maggot's bottom, Auntie Aggie.'

Winnie picked up her wand. 'I'd better make the place smell right for aunties. Brace yourself, Wilbur. *Abracadabra!*'

And instantly the lovely comfortable smell of mildew and mould was replaced by the sweety-tweety-neaty smell of pink petally rosy-posy pong.

'Mrrow!' complained Wilbur, putting a paw to his nose.

'I know!' said Winnie. 'Here, have a clothes peg.'

'Winifred Isaspell Tabitha Charmaine Hortense, will you please open this pesky door?!' Auntie Aggie's voice made Winnie's house shake.

'Deep breath, Wilbur. I'm going to let her in.'

192

Auntie Aggie seemed to fill the house
with pinkness. She looked at Winnie,
pointed at the clothes peg on her nose,
and said, 'What in the witchy world is
that for?'

'Oh, didn't you dow dat dese are da
noo fashion?' said Winnie.

'How silly you young people are!' said
Auntie Aggie. 'Take it off at once!'

193

'Yes, Auntie Aggie,' said Winnie.

Auntie Aggie pulled a hanky from her
sleeve, spat on it, then wiped it over
Winnie's face.

'Yeuch, get off!' said Winnie.

'I've come to sort you out, young lady,'
said Auntie Aggie.

'But I don't—' began Winnie.

'Don't argue!' said Auntie Aggie. 'Now,
where to begin?' She looked around the
kitchen and tutted. 'Dear, oh dear!' She
bent over, sticking her large pink-frocked
bottom in the air, as she took rubber
gloves from her bag, and pulled them on.

195

Then she waved her wipe-clean between-every-wish wand. 'Spit spot!' she commanded, and instantly all Winnie's stuff leapt up onto shelves and into cupboards.

Slam-slam-slam went the cupboard doors.

'Now I won't know where anything *is!*' wailed Winnie.

'Nonsense!' said Auntie Aggie. 'I'll smarten you up next.'

'But I don't—' began Winnie.

'Spit spot!' went Auntie Aggie, and instantly Winnie was swallowed in a smart business suit and her hair neatly styled.

Wilbur was tittering into his paws. 'Me-he-he-ow!'

Auntie Aggie looked at Wilbur. 'That stinky cat has got to be changed!' she said, and she raised her wipe-clean-between-every-wish wand and—

'No!' said Winnie. She leapt towards Wilbur, but her suit skirt was tight and her legs went **wang!** and she fell **bang!** onto the floor.

Suddenly Wilbur wasn't a cat any more.

'What have you done, you silly old
sponge pudding?' wailed Winnie. 'Where's
my Wilbur?'

'He's become a sweet little clean little
wabbit,' said Auntie Aggie.

'But I want *Wilbur!*' wailed Winnie.
'My *Wilbur!* I'm a witch, not a magician!
Give Wilbur back!'

'Er . . . no,' said Auntie Aggie. 'You young people don't know what's best. You'll soon love Wilbur the wabbit more than you ever loved that stinky cat. He can live in a nice pink cage.'

'Never!' said Winnie. She was gazing into the wabbit's eyes. She could see real Wilbur trapped inside the silly face with floppy ears.

Auntie Aggie wagged a plump finger at her. 'You wait, Winifred. When I'm an old witch I won't have the energy or magic to help you like this, and then you'll be sorry!'

Twitter-twee twitter-twee.

'It's my phone,' said Auntie Aggie. 'I'll take it outside and be back in a jiffy.'

Out bustled Auntie Aggie.

'Don't panic, Wilbur!' said Winnie. 'I'll
have you out of there in one snail-second,
but first I'm going to magic Auntie
Aggie!'

'Snuffle?' asked Wilbur.

'Yes,' said Winnie. 'Did you hear Auntie Aggie say that she'd not be able to do magic on us once she's an old lady? So I'm going to turn her into an old lady, just for as long as she stays here. Then I'll get you back, my Wilbur, my friend, my companion cat!'

As Auntie Aggie came back into the room, reaching for her wipe-clean-between-every-wish wand, Winnie waved her own wand. She shut her eyes tight and wished with all her might, 'Make Auntie Aggie much much older than me—*Abracadabra!*'

Gasp! went Auntie Aggie.

Gasp-nibble! went Wilbur the wabbit.

'Waaaaaaa!' went a little Winnie baby on the floor.

Wilbur glared at Winnie's wand, but

there was nothing wrong with the wand's
magic. Auntie Aggie *was* much much older
than Winnie, because Winnie had gone
backwards and become her baby self!

'Is that you, Winnie?' said Auntie Aggie.

She moved towards the door. 'Oo, I can't abide babies! Noisy smelly nasty things! I had to wait so many many years until you were old enough for me to work on you, Winnie, and now look what you've done!'

'Waaaaa!' went baby Winnie, kicking her legs and waving her fists. Then suddenly baby Winnie went quiet. A look of concentration came over her face. And a stinky smell filled the room.

'**Poooooey!** Ooo, dear!' said Auntie
Aggie. 'Quick, where's that clothes peg?
That's it, I'm off!' And off she went,
grabbing her bags and hurrying out of
Winnie's house and away.

205

Meanwhile, baby Winnie had got on to her hands and knees and was crawling at top speed out of the door.

Snuffle-nibble! went Wilbur the wabbit, but baby Winnie took no notice. So Wilbur the wabbit struggled with silly paws to pick up Winnie's wand.

Then he hopped the wand all over the lawn—boing! boing!—hopping in the shape of an '*A*' and—boing! boing!—in the shape of a '*b*' and then an '*r*' . . . until he'd spelled out the whole of *Abracadabra!*

Then, instantly, Winnie was back to her old self.

'Wilbur, you're a genius!' she said. Then she waved the wand. '*Abracadabra!*'

And instantly Wilbur was back to being proper Wilbur the cat again.

'Meow!' said Wilbur. 'Meow meow meow!'

'I know,' said Winnie. 'I'll be more careful what I wish for next time! But I don't think we'll see Auntie Aggie for a while!' Winnie patted Wilbur's tatty head. 'Oo, Wilbur, I'm so very very glad you're not really a wabbit!'

WINNIE
Goes Cleaning

''Tishoo!' *Sniff-sniff*, went Wilbur.

'Use that bat as a hanky,' said Winnie.
'What d'you want for lunch?'

Wilbur opened his mouth, but no
sound came out.

'You've lost your voice!' said Winnie.
'I know a cure for that!' Winnie opened
cupboards. She grabbed this and that and
a few of those.

Chop, slice, grate, bash, squeeze, slurp-slop, ready for the oven.

'Out of the way, Wilbur! I need a rack to stretch it on.'

But Wilbur didn't move fast enough. His tail was caught in the cupboard door.

Wilbur's fur stood on end, and he yelled a silent big **yeeeooowwl!**

He hit the ceiling then crashed to the floor. His tail was bent and there was a large lump on his head. Wilbur's mouth opened in a pitiful silent meow.

'Blooming heck!' said Winnie. She wiped sticky hands down her front and went to fetch her first aid box.

'Nice fresh leeches?' she said, but Wilbur shook his head hard. 'Just crushed earwigs for the headache and a bandage, then,' said Winnie.

Winnie found something to use as a splint. She wound sticky plaster round Wilbur's tail to hold the splint in place.

'There!' she said. 'I'm good at this, aren't I? I should have been a doctor instead of a witch!'

215

Later, down in the village, Winnie noticed something outside the school.

CLEANING OPERATIVE *Urgently required for village school* →

'Cleaning Operative urgently required for village school'

'Ooo, look, Wilbur!' said Winnie. 'It says . . .' Winnie ran a finger slowly along the word beginning with 'O'. '"O." "P." "E." "R . . ."' It says "operations", doesn't it? Ooo, Wilbur, they want somebody to do operations! Here's my chance to be a doctor!'

G
TIVE
uired
eschool

Wilbur put out a paw to try and grab
hold of Winnie's cardigan, but Winnie was
already at the door, pushing a button and
talking to the wall.

'You again!' said Mrs Parmar, the school secretary, when she opened the door. 'I remember you from when you cooked our school dinner. Out!'

'But I've come for the job,' said Winnie.

Mrs Parmar sagged. 'Well,' she sighed. 'I am desperate.'

'Where does it hurt?' asked Winnie.

'Don't touch me!' said Mrs Parmar. 'Just follow me.'

Mrs Parmar gave Winnie a pinny to wear.

'Here's your equipment,' she said, opening a cupboard.

'Really?' said Winnie. 'I can understand the bucket, but when does a doctor need spray polish?'

'Doctor?' boomed Mrs Parmar. 'The job is for a *cleaner*!'

'You want to waste my skills on dusting?' said Winnie.

'Oh, please do it, Winnie!' said Mrs Parmar, suddenly wilting. 'It's Parents' Evening tonight. If the school isn't clean they'll all take their children away and the school will close and I'll be out of a job and I'll have no money and I'll have to live in a cardboard box and I'll starve so thin I'll slip down the drain grating and then the sewer rats will get me and they'll nibble me and I don't like being nibbled and . . .'

'I don't like being nibbled myself, Mrs Parmar,' said Winnie. 'I'll do it.'

'Marvellous!' said Mrs Parmar. 'Everywhere must be clean by the end-of-school time.'

'Easy-peasy lemon squeezy!' said Winnie.

220

221

'I don't think much of this kind of broom,' said Winnie. 'Where's my proper broom, Wilbur?'

Winnie's broom swept double-quick. It brushed floors and walls and ceilings. It even tried to brush teachers' hair.

'Sorry about that!' said Winnie.

At last everywhere was clean except for the Hall.

'Come on, Wilbur,' said Winnie, and she barged into the Hall with her mop and bucket and dusters and vacuum cleaner and sprays. The Hall was full of children sitting on the floor. They turned and smiled at Winnie. Winnie smiled back.

'Hello, little ordinaries!' said Winnie.

223

But the head teacher was standing in front of the children, and he didn't smile. He pointed at Winnie.

'OUT!' he said.

'But Mrs Parmar said . . .' began Winnie.

'OUT!' said the head teacher again. So Winnie and Wilbur shuffled out of the Hall.

'Now how are we going to get the cleaning done in time?' asked Winnie.

Wilbur shrugged.

'I know!' said Winnie. 'I'll do a spell to make myself invisible! Then I can clean and they won't see me. Where's my wand?'

They looked in the bucket of dirty water, in Winnie's pockets, under Winnie's hat.

'I've lost my wand! I've lost my magic!?' wailed Winnie.

Then she had a thought. 'Ooo, I've remembered something from when I was little, Wilbur,' she said. 'I don't need magic to be invisible! I just need to cover my eyes with my hands. Come on, we'll go through the back door to the Hall so that the head teacher doesn't see the door opening. Hey, do you think they have arm and leg teachers as well as a head one, Wilbur?'

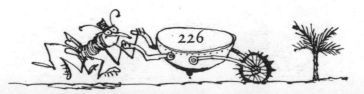

With a hand over her eyes, Winnie lugged the vacuum cleaner and the ladder and all the other bits into the Hall, behind the head teacher. The children laughed.

'Yes,' said the head teacher, not turning round. 'Yes, my story was rather amusing, wasn't it! Let me tell you another about the time I . . .' On he went with his boring story while the children laughed more and more. They cried. They held their tummies. There was even a puddle on the floor because they were laughing so much. On went the head teacher, but what the children were really laughing at was Winnie.

With a hand over her eyes, Winnie couldn't see anything. She tried to spray and polish the curtain, thinking it was a window.

'I'll have a go at those cobwebs next, Wilbur,' whispered Winnie.

She put the ladder up against the curtain
and began to climb, still with one hand over
her eyes. It was only Wilbur, holding with all
his catty might, who stopped the ladder from
crashing to the ground. Then Winnie bent
over, and she showed her witchy bloomers.

'Yay!' cheered the children.

'What?' said Winnie, taking her hand
from her face and realizing that she was
balanced in the air. 'Oh, gnats' knickers!
Don't let go, Wilbur! Ooooo! Noooo!'

CRASH! Wilbur wobbled, the ladder
fell, and so did Winnie . . . right into the
head teacher's arms.

'Hooray!' shouted the children, and they
clapped and cheered.

The mess was terrible.

230

'Oh, where where where is my wand?'
wailed Winnie . . . and suddenly she
remembered. 'Your tail, Wilbur!'

Winnie grabbed the end of the sticky
plaster on Wilbur's tail and she pulled.

'YEEEEOOWWL!' yelled Wilbur,
clutching his tail that was now balder than
the head teacher's head.

But Winnie had her wand back and she waved it around the room.

'Abracadabra!'

And instantly the place was tidy. The glass glinted, the floor gleamed, and the head teacher smiled.

'There!' said Winnie. 'All clean, *and* you've got your voice back, Wilbur. It's not every witch who can multi-task like that, you know!'

WINNIE
and the
Ghost in the Post

'I want that!' said Winnie, pointing to the telly. A smarmy vampire was lovingly holding up a pen in the shape of a mini broomstick.

'This pen can be yours!' said the vampire. He seemed to be gazing straight into Winnie's eyes.

'Can it really?' said Winnie. 'How's that then?'

The vampire chuckled and winked.

'This pen is no ordinary pen. No! This pen doesn't need to be pushed over the paper. This pen will do the writing for you!'

'Ooo, that's wonderful!' said Winnie, clasping her hands together. 'Isn't it wonderful, Wilbur? Just what I need!'

Wilbur wasn't listening. He was busy writing a shopping list.

Eyes of newts

The vampire went on, 'This pen is the prize for our new poetry competition. Send in your poem and we'll choose which of you will win the pen.'

'Oo!' said Winnie, jumping up. 'Where's a pencil? Where's a bit of paper? I've got to get poetic, and you've got to help me, Wilbur!'

Wilbur glanced at Winnie's feet, then he wrote:

Polish for boots

Winnie waved her wand.

'*Abracadabra!*'

Instantly there appeared piles of paper and stacks of pens.

'I'm all ready!' she said. 'Now, what shall I put for my poem? I know! "The cat sat on the mat".'

Wilbur rolled his eyes.

A packet of tea

'But it's true,' said Winnie. 'Poetry should be about truth! You are a cat and you are sitting on a mat!'

Winnie tried to write down 'cat' and 'mat', but she couldn't even manage that.

'Oh, earwig belly buttons! You see,
that's why I need that pen! Pleeeease write
it for me, Wilbur!'

But Wilbur was still busy with his list.

Some fish for me

'Oh, my talents are wasted, that's what
they are!' Winnie tugged at her hair. 'If
only somebody would write down my
poem!'

Then Winnie had a thought. 'Oh, I know, I'll get one of those ghost writers!' she said. 'Where's that website for ghosts by post? Here it is!'

Winnie clicked the mouse to make the computer talk to her.

'PLEASE ANSWER THE FOLLOWING,' said the computer.

'KIND OF GHOST REQUIRED:

1) TO SCARE UNWANTED GUESTS

A) DRAGGING CLANKING CHAINS

B) HEADLESS

C) MOANING GREY WOMAN

2) TO ATTRACT VISITORS TO HISTORIC BUILDINGS

(A) , (B) , OR (C) , AS ABOVE.

3) TO DO SOME WRITING FOR YOU

A) THRILLERS

B) ROMANCES

C) POETRY'

'Definitely a 3(c),' said Winnie. 'Although I might try a 1(b) next time Auntie Aggie comes to stay!'

'Size of ghost wanted

1) small

2) medium

3) large'

Winnie click-ticked (1). 'A small one can write as well as a big one, and it'll cost less.'

She got Wilbur to fill in the address.

Send to: Winnie the Witch, 13 Bat's Wing Crescent, Little Rats Bottom, LO1 3KP.

Winnie sent the form by witchmail,
which is fast. Next instant there was a
snap of the letter box and a slim envelope
fell onto the doormat.

'My ghost in the post!' said Winnie.

Wilbur sniffed the envelope, and hissed.
The envelope seemed to be breathing.

Winnie the Witch
13 Batswing Crescent
Little Rats Bottom
LOI 3KP

'Give it to me!' said Winnie. She tore
open the envelope, and tipped out . . .

'It looks like an old hanky!' said
Winnie, disappointed. 'Is it dead?' She
poked at the white thing. 'Oo, no it isn't!
Look, Wilbur!'

The flat white thing quivered. Then it rose elegantly into the air and bowed to Winnie and then to Wilbur.

'Good afternoooon!' it said. 'I am your poetic spooook. What do you desire me to doooooo?'

'Oh, dear little Post Ghost!' said Winnie. 'May I call you PG? I just want you to write a poem to win a competition.'

PG shuddered. 'Did you say *"just* write a poem"?'

'Er . . . yes,' said Winnie.

'My dear modom,' said PG in a quivering voice. 'There is no "just" about writing a poem.' PG put his ghostly hand to his ghostly brow. 'I have to be inspired before I can write!'

Winnie the Witch
13 Bat's Wing Caveau
Little Rat's Bottom
LOTS R.I.P.

247

'Have you?' said Winnie. 'How do we do that then?'

'Show me something beauooootiful,' said PG.

Winnie simpered and patted her hair.

PG pulled a face to show that he didn't think Winnie fitted the bill.

'What about Wilbur then?' said Winnie. 'Wilbur's beautiful. I'd like a poem about him.'

'I couldn't write about a smelly old
cat!' PG looked around the room. 'Dear,
oh dear. Nothing at all that I could
uoooooooose. Is there, outside, perhaps,
a lovely viewoooooo? Glistening with
dewoooo? That would doooooo.'

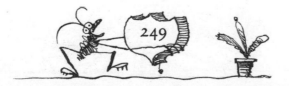

'Ooo, I can hear the poem coming already!' said Winnie, excited. 'Come outside, PG.'

It was a sunny day, but . . .

'I have it!' said PG. 'Hand me my quill.' He began to write—

Oh, moooon, moooon

Beauooootiful moooon!

'You sound like a cow with belly ache!' said Winnie.

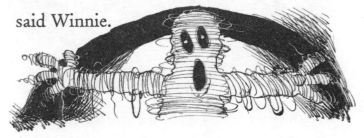

The little ghost flounced. *Sniff.* 'I *was* going to go on with, "You look like a silver spoooon". But I can't create when I'm upset. I'm sensitive. I need ambiance and atmosphere and appreciation to doooo my work . . .'

'Oh, I'm ever so sorry!' said Winnie.
'It's just that I haven't been to school and I
don't know much about poetry. I'll shut
up, shall I?'

So PG wrote about June (even though it
was April) and a balloon and a tune. And
Winnie tried very hard not to yawn.

251

Meanwhile, Wilbur was ready to go shopping.

'Ooo, wait, Wilbur!' called Winnie. 'I've got to put my poem in the post. And PG's got to be sent back toooo. And I do just need to go to the loooo before we go. Oh, heck, poetry seems to be catching!'

Winnie stuffed the poem into one envelope and the ghost into another.

'Quick! Let's get them posted!'

In the shop, Winnie and Wilbur looked
at their shopping list. It said—

Oh, moooon, moooon,

Beauooootiful moooon!

'Oh, newts' nosedrops!' said Winnie.

'We've posted the wrong bit of paper!'

So Winnie and Wilbur went home feeling cross. They slumped on sofas and switched on the telly. There was the vampire with the smile, just announcing . . .

'The winner of our pen competition is . . . Winnie the Witch!'

'Oh! Oh! Oh!' Winnie was jumping up and down as if she'd got ants in her pants. 'I won!'

The vampire read the winning poem:

'Eyes of newts

Polish for boots

A bag of tea

Some fish for me

Swede for the stew

A smell-fresh for the loo.'

'It's those "ooo" sounds that make this a truly poetic poem,' said the vampire. 'Well done, Winnie.'

Wilbur cleared his throat. He pointed a claw at himself.

'Oh, yes,' said Winnie. 'You wrote that, Wilbur. But will you still let me use the pen? Pretty please?'

The first thing Winnie used the pen-
that-writes-on-its-own for was to write a
poem for Wilbur.

The fat cat sat on the mat
He isn't a bat or even a rat
He is Wilbur, my cat
And I love him for that!

Mini
WINNIE

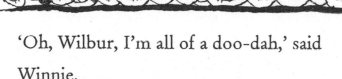

'Oh, Wilbur, I'm all of a doo-dah,' said
Winnie.

'Mrow?' asked Wilbur.

He was mashing worms, ready for tea.

'Wendy's coming round. I've ripped my
dress trying to reach for the best croakery
in the top cupboard. I've got nothing
smart to wear now, and you know what
Wendy's like!'

Winnie pulled all her pockets inside out to reveal a grey bit of slug gum and a couple of cross snails.

'I've not got any money, so I can't buy anything new. And, anyway, look at the clock! There's no time!' Winnie stroked her chin. 'Hmmn,' she said. 'But I have got a lot of old clothes in the attic. They say that fashions come around if you give them time. Come on, Wilbur! Let's see what we can find!'

Winnie pushed open the attic trapdoor and pulled down the attic ladder, and up she went. The attic was hot and dark and full of boxes and bags and suitcases. 'You use the torch, Wilbur, and I'll use the jar of glow-worms. See what you can find.'

Wilbur opened drawers and doors while
Winnie stuck her bottom in the air and
searched in bags and boxes. Soon there
were hats and hankies, bats and slippers,
books and flippers flying everywhere.

'Aha!' said Winnie, waving something.
'Mreow?'

'Oo, look, Wilbur! The shoes I wore on the day I fell in the duck pond! And the poncho I wore to that witches' disco. And see this? I bought it in a sale at Witch Wardrobe, but I've never worn it. That might do nicely, don't you think?' Winnie thrust a musty dusty fusty old skirt with labels still on it at Wilbur.

Wilbur stepped back.

'Meowatichoo!' he sneezed.

Winnie took a sniff.

''choo!' she went. She gave the skirt a shake and some purple and yellow moths flew out of it.

Wilbur was washing, licking a paw and then wiping the paw over his head.

'Heck, I need a wash too!' said Winnie, brushing cobwebs off her cardigan. Winnie licked her hand, then wiped it over her head, then licked it again.

'Yuck!' she said. 'I don't know what cat tastes like, Wilbur, but witch tastes disgusting!' She stuck out her tongue and licked the skirt. 'Euch! All hairy! It's like licking a Highland cow!'

Winnie bundled all the old clothes together. 'They can have a bath with me.'

Winnie ran a bath and tipped in frogspawn bubble bath. She threw in the clothes. Then she got in herself and sploshed around.

'Tra la la! Are you coming in too, Wilbur?'

'Mrrow!'

Winnie and Wilbur hung the clothes on
the line, clipping them in place with baby
alligators.

'Yeeow!' yelled Winnie. 'These pegs
bite!'

Then they went inside for a snack of
elephants' toenail crisps and eel slime tea.

'How long do clothes take to dry?' asked Winnie.

Wilbur shook his head and pointed out of the window.

'Oh, cockroach crusts!' said Winnie. 'It's raining!'

Winnie waved her wand angrily at the window.

'Abracadabra!'

Instantly the rain stopped. The grey clouds went. The sun came out and a gentle wind blew.

'Perfect for drying,' said Winnie.

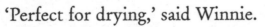

But the wind began to blow harder. It blew so hard the birds couldn't cling to the trees. Winnie's knickers were in knots, her tights in a tangle, her dress in a mess, and her cardigan in a—

'Blooming heck!' said Winnie.

It blew so hard that the big man next door's washing came flying over.

'Cor, look at that!' said Winnie.

But Winnie's washing was escaping too.
Wilbur ran outside and tried to catch the
vests and socks, the bonnets and skirts.

'Abracadabra!' shouted Winnie,
waving her wand. The wind stopped, but
it was too late. Winnie's washing had
fallen, splish-splosh, into muddy puddles.

'Oh, botherarmarations!' said Winnie.
'Put them all in the washing machine,
Wilbur.'

Winnie filled the machine drawer with
flea powder.

'Stand back!' said Winnie.

She pushed the button and . . .

kerpowowowowow! The machine
coughed and collapsed. It spat out washing
and springs and powder all over the place.

'Fleas' flippers! We'll have to do a proper witch wash. Quick!' said Winnie, looking at her watch. 'Where's the big cauldron?'

They put water and powder and the clothes into the cauldron. Wilbur found sticks and Winnie lit a fire. Then they both stirred the pot with old wands. Steam began to rise. The water began to bubble and boil.

'That'll get them clean,' said Winnie.

The clothes did get clean, but . . .

'They've shrunk!' wailed Winnie. 'I
won't fit in any of them! I'm too blooming
big! Pass my wand over, Wilbur.'

Winnie pointed the wand at herself.

'Abracadabra!' she shouted.

And in an instant there was empty air
where Winnie had been the moment
before. And there, on the floor, was a mini
Winnie, no bigger than a teaspoon with
scruffy hair.

'Ooer,' said mini Winnie. 'Aren't spiders BIG!
But at least I can wear the clothes now!'

Winnie tried on this . . . and that . . .
and those. 'This is the outfit, I think, Wilbur. Look
at the clock! I must make the tea.'

But mini Winnie couldn't reach the
work surface or the tap or the teapot. She
tried climbing up a chair leg. She tried
swinging up on the kettle flex.

'**Brrriiing!** Let me in!'

'It's the dooryell!' said mini Winnie. 'Wendy's
here! Quick! Where's that wand? *Abracadabra!*'

273

Instantly Winnie was back to normal size.
And standing in just her undies.

'Oh, double-heck!' she shrieked.

'Brriiing brriiing! Let me in!'

'What shall I do, Wilbur?' panicked Winnie.

Wilbur handed Winnie the patchwork
tea cosy.

'It's too small to cover me!' said Winnie. 'And,
anyway, which bit of me goes through which
hole?'

But Wilbur was shaking his head and
pointing.

'Oh, I see!' said Winnie. 'Brillamaroodle
idea, Wilbur!'

Winnie quickly pointed her wand at the
pile of tiny clothes.

'Abracadabra!' she shouted, stirring
the clothes together into a sparkling whirl
that settled to reveal one new dress; a
patchwork dress that used all Winnie's
very favourite old clothes from all time.
'Oh, I love it!' said Winnie, slipping the
dress on. 'A perfect fit!'

'**Brrrriiiingg!** Are you deaf, you silly witch?' yelled the dooryell.

'Coming!' said Winnie.

In came Wendy, bursting out of a tight brand-new outfit. 'Do you like it, Win?' she said. 'I bought it this morning from Frights. I suppose you're in your usual . . . oh!'

She stopped still. 'You're wearing something new! Where's it from?'

'From W & W,' said Winnie, doing a twirl. 'Do you like it?'

'Well, it is . . . um . . . unusual,' said Wendy. 'You know, there is something strangely familiar about it.'

'Never mind that,' said Winnie. 'Come and have some pond tea and toasted toadstools.'

And they all had tea together.

AND FINALLY . . .

Where do ghosts
buy stamps?

At the ghost
office.

Who keeps a watch
for ghost ships?

The ghost guard.

278

What happens to authors
when they die?

They become
ghost writers.

How does a ghost
go through a locked door?

With a skeleton key.

What did father
ghost say to his
little boy?

Spook when
you're
spoken to.

What do sea monsters eat?
Fish and ships

What's big and green and sits in the corner
all day looking miserable?

The incredible sulk.

What's a monster's favourite TV programme?
BeastEnders.

What monster
lives in your
nose?

A bogeyman.

Which monster runs around Paris in a plastic bag?

The lunch-pack of Notre Dame.

Interviewer: Do you like children?

Monster: Oh yes, I love children — boiled, fried, scrambled . . .

What's very large, yellow, lives in Scotland and has never been seen?

The Loch Ness Canary.

What do monsters make with cars?

Traffic jam.

Where do you find vampire snails?

On the ends of vampires' fingers.

What do you call a blood-drinking sheep?

A lambpire.

Where does Dracula stay when he goes to New York?
In the Vampire State Building.

283

Doctor, doctor, I think I'm shrinking.

Well, you'll just have to be a little patient.

Doctor, doctor, I keep thinking
I'm a park of cards.

Sit down, I'll deal with you later.

Doctor, doctor, I think
I'm a pair of curtains.

Well, pull yourself together.

Doctor, doctor, I've lost my memory.

When did it happen?

When did
what happen?

Doctor, doctor, my wooden leg
is giving me a lot of pain.

Why's that?

May wife keeps hitting me
on the head with it.

Doctor, doctor,
I think I need glasses.

You certainly do.
This is a fish and chip shop.

Wilbur

Winnie the Witch

Wanda

The Head Teacher

The Little Ordinaries

Wayne

Mrs Parmar

Jerry the Giant

The Toof Fairy

The Conductor

The Shopkeeper

Wendy

Auntie Aggie

Enjoy more magic moments with
Winnie AND Wilbur